DANGER!
A GIFT FOR
Charlie
"little kitty"
From
Grammie Witch Sonnie
I love you very much.
xoxoxo
BEWARE
DO NOT
DELIVERY

Published by Hallmark Books,
a division of Hallmark Cards, Inc.,
Kansas City, MO 64141
Visit us on the Web at www.Hallmark.com.

Editorial Director: Todd Hafer
Editor: Theresa Trinder
Art Director: Kevin Swanson
Designer: Mary Eakin
Production Artist: Dan Horton

ISBN: 978-1-59530-213-7
BOK6126
Printed and bound in China

A Case of the Creepy Crawlies

written by Keely Chace
illustrated by Jeanne Rittmueller

GIFT BOOKS
from Hallmark

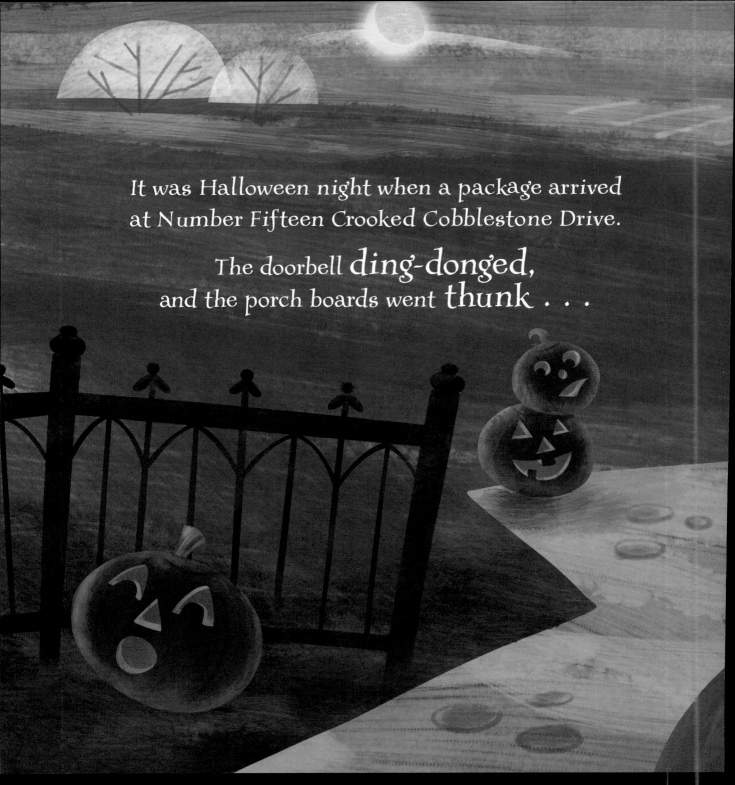

It was Halloween night when a package arrived
at Number Fifteen Crooked Cobblestone Drive.

The doorbell ding-donged,
and the porch boards went thunk . . .

when someone (or something)
dropped off the big trunk.

No. 15

The **rickety racket**
awoke little Willow,
the wee witch who'd been
fast asleep on her pillow.

She slinked down the hall like some wee, sneaky beast,
not afraid of the dark, not alarmed in the least.

Home
Sweet
Home

Past her grandwitch's room,
past the old clock **tick-tocking**,
Willow crept to the door,
where she thought she heard **knocking**.

She slid back the dead bolt,
threw open the door . . .

but no one was there.
Just a crate.
Nothing more.

She thought, What in the world?
Who had left this so late?
Who is it for?
What's in this old crate?

Willow shoved it inside using all her wee might.
It went BUMP through the door
and crrrreeeak in the night.

She climbed up to see
how this package got packed.
It sure was a mysterious case
to be cracked!

Was it candy? Enough to last clear to next fall?
It didn't smell tasty or sweet. (Not at all!)

Or maybe a broomstick that flew twice as fast?
A digital spell-casting wand? What a blast!

Maybe Gran sent away
for some potion supplies.
She said she'd been needing
a jar of newts' eyes.

Or was it some hairs
from the head of a flea?
No, it might not be that . . .
But what could it BE?

What if (just what if)
something bad lurked inside?
Something creepy and crawly
with jaws a mile wide?

Maybe a mummy with curses to fling?
A snakey-haired goblin?
EEEEK! What WAS this thing?

A troll with a toothache?
A ninety-pound spider?
Willow sprang from the crate
as chills rose inside her.

CREEEEAK

SSCRATC

SSSSSSSS

RR

Was that **scratching** she heard?
Did it want to get out?
Willow tried to stay calm,
but she let out a SHOUT.

Forget being brave!
She turned and she ran!
She ran in the dark!
And **smacked** right into . . .

GRAN!

"Oh, it's too scary!
Don't look!" Willow shrieked.
But Gran just said,
"Hmm . . . let's have us a peek."

Willow wasn't so sure, but she took her Gran's hand.
They went straight to the crate, unlocked it, AND . . .

the lid creaked right open.
It gave a slight glow.
Willow peeked in.
And what do you know?

The thing she was scared of,
that gave her such fright,
that was plunked on her doorstep
so late in the night,
had shiny green eyes
and was covered in fur!

And it leapt from the box!
And it started to . . .

puuurrrrrrr.

Though she might have been scared,
it worked out in the end.

Every good little witch
needs a good little friend.

If you have enjoyed this book,
we would love to hear from you.

Please send your comments to:
Hallmark Book Feedback
P.O. Box 419034
Mail Drop 215
Kansas City, MO 64141

Or e-mail us at:
booknotes@hallmark.com